Meow!
Will you answer
the call for adventure?

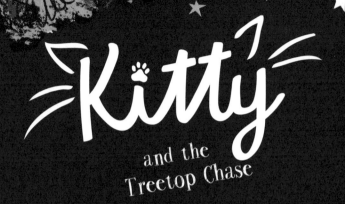

Kitty

and the
Treetop Chase

 Greenwillow Books
An Imprint of HarperCollinsPublishers

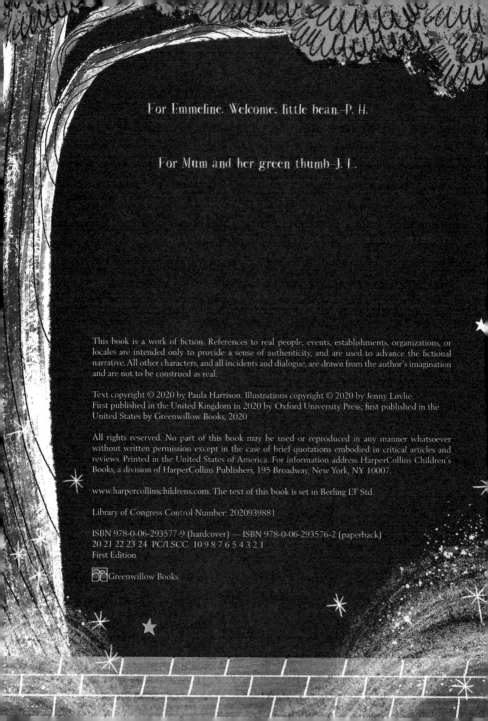

For Emmeline. Welcome. little bean.–P. H.

For Mum and her green thumb–J. L.

Text copyright © 2020 by Paula Harrison. Illustrations copyright © 2020 by Jenny Løvlie
First published in the United Kingdom in 2020 by Oxford University Press; first published in the United States by Greenwillow Books, 2020

www.harpercollinschildrens.com. The text of this book is set in Berling LT Std.

Library of Congress Control Number: 2020939881

ISBN 978-0-06-293577-9 (hardcover) — ISBN 978-0-06-293576-2 (paperback)
20 21 22 23 24 PC/LSCC 10 9 8 7 6 5 4 3 2 1
First Edition

Greenwillow Books

Contents

Meet Kitty & Her Cat Crew

Kitty

Kitty has special powers—but is she ready to be a superhero just like her mom?

Luckily, Kitty's cat crew has faith in her and shows Kitty the hero that lies within.

Pumpkin

A stray ginger kitten who is utterly devoted to Kitty.

Figaro

Wise and kind, Figaro knows the neighborhood like the back of his paw.

Pixie

Pixie has a nose for trouble and whiskers for mischief!

Katsumi

Sleek and sophisticated, Katsumi is quick to call Kitty at the first sign of trouble.

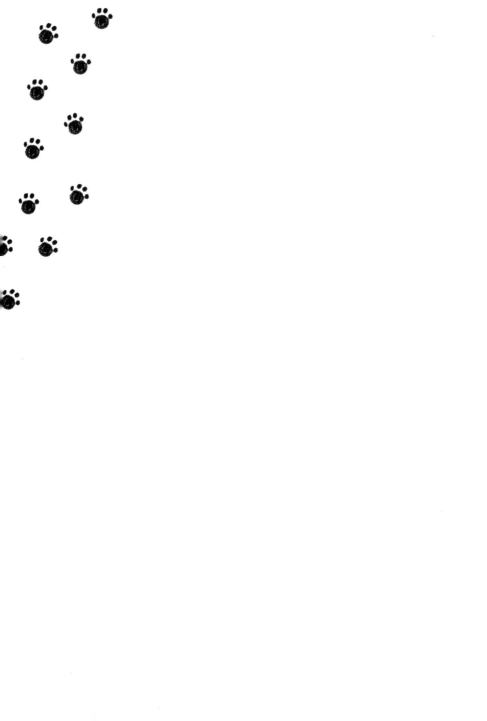

Kitty

and the
Treetop Chase

Chapter 1

"There you are, Pumpkin! That looks just like you." Kitty drew the last whisker onto her cat picture and showed it to Pumpkin.

She had drawn a plump little ginger cat with bright eyes and a stripy tail.

Pumpkin jumped onto the table to take a closer look. "It's me!" he purred, rubbing his furry head against Kitty's arm. "I really like it."

"I'll put it up on the wall," said Kitty, smiling.

She and Pumpkin had been best friends ever since she'd rescued him from a tall clock tower. Kitty had cat-like superpowers, and she was learning to become a real superhero. Sometimes she went on adventures in the moonlight with her cat crew. She loved climbing and balancing on the rooftops, and using her special nighttime vision and super hearing to spot when trouble was coming.

Most of all, Kitty loved being able to talk to animals, especially to Pumpkin,

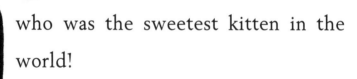

who was the sweetest kitten in the world!

Kitty stuck the picture of Pumpkin on the wall and stood back to admire it. Then she noticed a delicious scent drifting out of the kitchen. Pumpkin's nose started twitching, too.

"That smells lovely!" said Kitty. "I wonder if Mom's doing some baking."

She ran into the kitchen, where Mom was taking a large cake pan out of the oven. "Have you made a cake? Mmm . . . smells like chocolate!"

"There's nothing wrong with your super senses!" Mom laughed. "Yes, I've made a special cake because we have visitors coming to stay tonight.

Some very good friends have just moved to Hallam City, and they have a son who's your age."

"Oh! What's his name?" asked Kitty.

Mom lifted the cake out of the cake pan and a cloud of chocolaty steam filled the kitchen. "His name is Ozzy. You could have a sleepover in the new tree house, if you like." She gave Kitty a funny smile. "I'm sure you'll find that you have a lot in common."

Kitty hesitated. Dad had built the tree house in the garden last week, and it was meant to belong only to her since her brother, Max, was too young to be allowed up the ladder on his own. She wasn't sure she wanted to share it with anyone else.

Ding-dong went the doorbell.

"That must be them now!" Kitty's mom put down her oven mitts. "I hope they're hungry."

Kitty's forehead wrinkled as her mom hurried to the door. Why had her mom said

7

that Kitty might have a lot in common with Ozzy? It seemed strange when she'd never met him before!

Kitty's mom called to her from the hall. "Kitty, come and meet everyone! These are my friends Molly and Neil Porter, and this is Ozzy." She pointed to a boy with curly dark hair and round glasses.

Kitty said hello while Pumpkin hid behind her legs. The Porters said hello back and smiled in a friendly way, but Ozzy just nodded awkwardly and fiddled with his glasses.

"Why don't you show everyone around, Kitty?" said her dad, coming into the hall. "Max and I will set the dinner table."

Kitty showed the Porters around the house, and they said how much they liked her room before asking her all about her school. Ozzy just followed them from room to room and didn't say a thing.

"This is terrible!" Kitty whispered to Pumpkin. "What if he doesn't speak for the whole sleepover?"

Pumpkin put his paw on Kitty's knee. "Don't worry," he whispered back. "I'll keep you company."

After they'd eaten dinner and had a slice of the chocolate cake, Kitty's mom turned to Ozzy with a smile. "I thought it might be fun for you and Kitty to have your sleepover in the tree house tonight. It's so much more exciting than sleeping indoors!"

"I can show you the tree house if you like," added Kitty, jumping up.

Ozzy followed Kitty out the

back door into the shadowy garden. Moonlight glinted on the windows and the silver watering can. The round garden lights cast a soft yellow glow across the flower beds, and a tiny breath of wind made the flowers sway and the trees rustle.

Kitty's dad had built the tree house in the big oak tree at the far end of the garden. A sturdy wooden ladder led up into the branches. Ozzy and Kitty climbed the rungs in silence.

"Here it is. I hope you like it!" Kitty

clambered into the little wooden house.
The place was quite roomy, and she had
set pots of marigolds on the windowsills
and hung a mobile of glittery stars from

the roof to make it pretty. Ozzy looked all around, blinking as he peered up at the starry mobile. Kitty wondered if he felt nervous about sleeping outside. "We don't have to sleep here if you don't want to. I know not everyone likes being outside in the dark . . ."

"I love being outside in the dark!" said Ozzy, his eyes lighting up suddenly. "Everything looks more interesting at night."

Kitty looked at him in surprise. At last he was talking to her! "That's great! Should we put on our pajamas and grab our comforters? Then we can start the sleepover right away."

Ozzy nodded, and they went back inside to change. Along with her comforter, Kitty fetched a small bag with a teddy bear and a book. She pushed her superhero suit into the bag, too. She never knew when she might need it!

Kitty's dad brought out two air beds for them to sleep on. Pumpkin followed Kitty up the ladder and they snuggled down under her comforter. Ozzy wriggled down under his own

comforter and stared around with wide, dark eyes.

Kitty gazed out of the tree house window at the moonlit garden. Her catlike night vision allowed her to see everything so clearly. Stars twinkled across the deep black sky, and a wisp of smoke curled out of the neighbor's chimney.

"It feels magical when there's a full moon, doesn't it?" Kitty asked.

Ozzy nodded and lay down. "I'm going to sleep now. Good night!"

Kitty tried to stay awake for a little while, although Pumpkin was already fast asleep beside her. The wind swirled around the garden, and the tree house

swayed gently
with the branches of the
oak tree. Kitty felt as if she was
being rocked to sleep, and at last her
eyelids drooped and she couldn't stay
awake anymore.

Chapter 2

Kitty woke to a tapping noise on the tree house window. She sat up, sleepily pushing her hair away from her face. It must be one of her cat crew calling her to go on an adventure. Perhaps Pixie had found a new place to explore, or maybe

Figaro had come to tell her someone was in trouble.

Pumpkin yawned and pricked up his ears. "What's that, Kitty? Is something happening?"

Kitty spotted Katsumi's honey-colored fur and serious dark eyes outside the window. She scrambled up and undid the latch. Ozzy didn't stir, so she kept her voice to a whisper. "Hello, Katsumi. Is everything all right?"

Katsumi sprang inside, her tail swaying. "There's a commotion at the bakery. The bakery owners got a new dog not long ago and he's jumping up and down, absolutely wrecking the place! I think we should go over there and stop him."

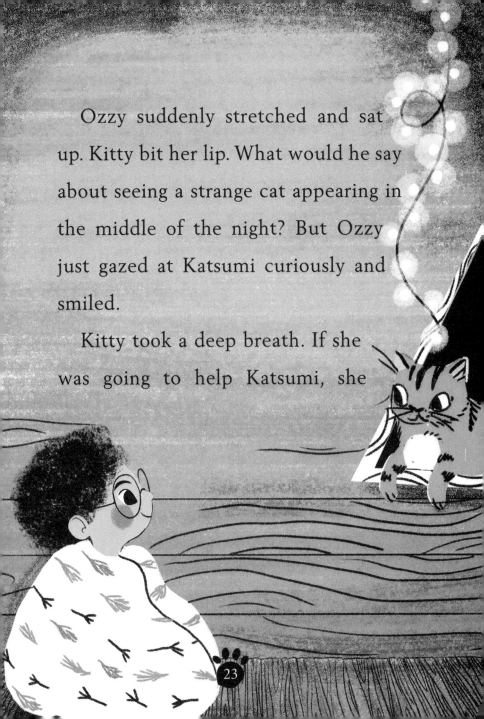

Ozzy suddenly stretched and sat up. Kitty bit her lip. What would he say about seeing a strange cat appearing in the middle of the night? But Ozzy just gazed at Katsumi curiously and smiled.

Kitty took a deep breath. If she was going to help Katsumi, she should explain to Ozzy where she was going. "Um . . . I have something to tell you. I'm a superhero with catlike powers! I often go on adventures in the moonlight, especially when someone needs my help. Katsumi just told me about an emergency."

"That's funny!" Ozzy smiled. "I'm a superhero, too." He leaned out of

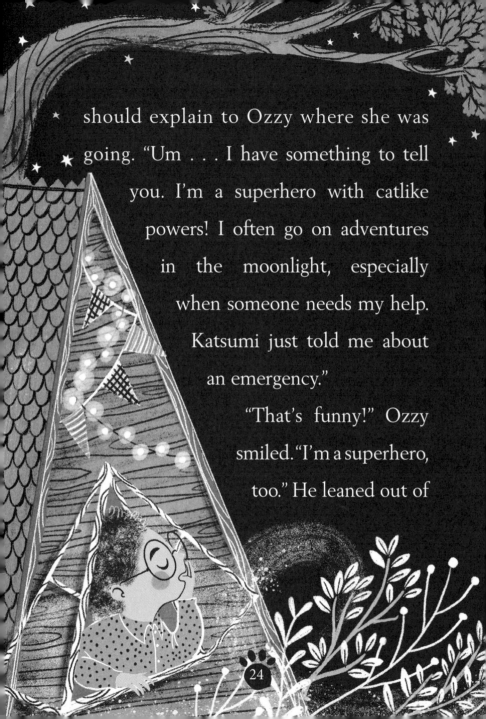

the window and made a long hooting sound.

"Really?" said Kitty doubtfully. "Then you have superpowers, like me?"

Ozzy nodded, still grinning, and a minute later, a snowy owl with beautiful downy feathers swooped out of the dark sky and settled on the windowsill. She squawked, and Ozzy stroked her head. "This is my new friend, Olive," he explained to Kitty. "I met her just after moving here to Hallam City."

Kitty stared in surprise. Then she remembered she didn't want to seem rude. "Hello, Olive. I'm Kitty, and this is Pumpkin and Katsumi."

Olive bobbed her head to each of them. "Ozzy is training to be a superhero, and his owl-like powers give him amazing eyesight and super hearing. When he's finished his training, he'll be unstoppable!" she said proudly. "We've

already had our first moonlit adventure together."

Ozzy pulled a brown

cloak lined with dark feathers from his sleepover bag. "I wear this cape, you see! The feathers let me swoop and glide just like an owl, and they're brilliant for camouflage! I have a mask, too." He put on his superhero outfit and a feathery mask. His eyes looked big and wide as he blinked at Kitty.

Kitty hunted inside her own bag before pulling out her black cape, cat ears, and mask. She put on her superhero outfit. For a long moment, Kitty and Ozzy stared at each other.

"Wow! A cape that lets you glide sounds great," Kitty said at last. "I spend a lot of time jumping and somersaulting, so I don't really need one of those."

"Most people wouldn't be able to use it properly anyway," Ozzy told her.

Kitty frowned. She was sure she'd be able to use a cape like that if she wanted to!

Ozzy quickly explained to Olive that there was a dog going wild in the bakery.

"I think we should hurry," urged Katsumi. "Who knows what this dog will do next?"

Kitty dashed to the door of the
tree house, with Pumpkin scampering
after her. "We can follow the rooftops.
I'll show you!"

"I think it would be better to use
the trees," replied Ozzy. "You know the
way, don't you Olive?"

"Yes, follow me!" Olive flew over the
fence and glided across the garden next
door.

"Oh! I guess we could do that." Kitty
climbed swiftly to the top of the tree,
with Katsumi close behind her. She

leaned down to help
Pumpkin, who was
struggling to reach
the next branch.
Ozzy clambered up
beside her, puffing a
little. He clutched the branches
tightly, wobbling as the tree
swayed in the wind.

"Will you be all right?"

31

Kitty felt her superpowers growing inside her. She knew she could easily leap to the next tree, but would Ozzy be able to keep up with her?

Ozzy grinned and spread out his feathered cape. "Of course I will! Watch

this." And he
leaped into the air. The wind
rippled through his cloak like a sail as
he silently glided to the next tree.

Kitty sprang after him, landing
perfectly in the treetop. Her catlike

powers tingled through her body like electricity. The jump to the next tree was even wider. Ozzy grinned at Kitty as he set off, swooping noiselessly through the air.

Kitty gathered Pumpkin into her arms. She knew the jump would be too much for the kitten. "Hold on tight!" she whispered, and Pumpkin clung to her shoulders, his stripy tail curled around her neck.

Kitty and Ozzy went on swooping and leaping from treetop to treetop.

Olive flew on
ahead while
Katsumi leaped
gracefully along
the branches. The
houses were dark and
the back gardens were only lit by
moonlight.

At last, Ozzy reached the last tree
and swooped to the ground. He landed
gracefully beside a hedge, almost
camouflaged by his cloak. Kitty sprang

onto a fence before somersaulting to
on the pavement.

"Nice moves!" Ozzy nodded.

"Thanks—you too!" Kitty smiled.

"We're here!" Katsumi nodded to the bakery on the opposite side of the street. "There was a terrible commotion earlier."

Kitty gazed at the storefront, which displayed a large pink sign: THE STICKY BUN BAKERY. She remembered coming here a few weeks ago to buy donuts. The owners, Mr. and Mrs. Gallo, had been very friendly.

Ozzy tilted his head a little, frowning intently as he stared through the bakery's dark windows. "It all seems quiet in there now. I think we should keep watch for a while and see if anything happens."

Kitty shook her head. "We need to find out what's going on! I'll go in by myself if you want."

Ozzy frowned. "No way! We should both go. I'll race you there!" He darted across the silent street, and Kitty ran after him. She was determined not to let him be the first one inside!

THE STICKY BUN

Chapter 3

Ozzy and Kitty rushed across the empty street. Katsumi and Pumpkin scampered after them, and Olive fluttered overhead. Moonlight glinted on the bakery sign and rows of cherry pies and pink-iced cupcakes stood on display close to the door. Kitty slipped around to the back and found an open window. She climbed onto the windowsill and peered in. It was dark inside.

"Be careful, Kitty!" Pumpkin's tail twitched nervously.

Slipping through the window, Kitty dropped to the floor and looked around. This was the kitchen, with rows of large ovens and shelves stacked with ingredients. There was no sign of the dog, but the work table was covered with white flour in such a thick layer, it looked as though it had snowed.

One shelf had fallen down, scattering cherries and raisins all over the floor. Kitty gaped at the mess. Why would the

dog have done this to his new home?

Ozzy tapped on the door. "Let us in, Kitty! What's going on in there?"

Kitty hurried to unlock the door, nearly tripping over an upside-down mixing bowl. "It's even worse than I expected. It looks as if a whole pack of animals jumped around in here!"

"Maybe he was really hungry and he

was searching for dog food," suggested Ozzy.

"Dogs can be such messy creatures! A bird would never do something like this." Olive settled on a counter and then clicked her beak crossly at the flour on her talons.

"I don't think he can be a very nice

dog," said Pumpkin nervously. "He's not lying in wait to pounce on us, is he?"

"I don't think so. Let's see if there are any clues in the shop." Kitty dashed down the corridor and gasped. A splendid three-tier cake with swirls of lemon-colored icing lay squashed on the floor. Katsumi, who had followed Kitty, shook her head.

"Poor Mr. and Mrs. Gallo! They're going to be so upset when they see what's happened," said Kitty. "We'd better find this dog before he causes even more trouble."

"There are paw prints here!" Ozzy pointed to the trail of sticky marks that led all over the shop. "If we follow them, they'll lead us straight to him."

Kitty looked closely at the paw prints. "It's this way!" She darted down the hallway into a storeroom with an odd doorway at one end.

"This must be where they deliver the sacks of flour," said Katsumi.

Kitty pushed the odd door and it swung open gently.

"We'll never get through there. It's too narrow," Ozzy told her.

"I can get through! Go back through the door and I'll meet you in the

yard." Crouching low, Kitty squeezed gracefully through the doorway and out the other side. Pumpkin and Katsumi followed her, and they found themselves in a small backyard leading to a side alley.

The sticky paw prints glinted in the moonlight. The trail led across the yard and over some empty boxes toward the alley.

A distant howl rose into the air, and the hairs on the back of Kitty's neck prickled. Was that the dog they were

looking for? She listened carefully, but the howling stopped and a thick silence settled over the bakery's backyard.

Ozzy ran out the back door. "Did you hear that? Sounds like this dog is still close by."

"Such a horrible noise!" Olive shuddered as she settled on Ozzy's shoulder.

Kitty suddenly wondered if the creature was dangerous. She didn't say anything to Ozzy. He already looked nervous—blinking and fiddling with his mask. She glanced at Katsumi, Pumpkin, and Olive. "At least there are five of us and we can look for the dog together. We'd better track him down before he causes even more damage!"

They hurried down the alley, following the trail of paw prints. The sticky prints soon faded, but Kitty spotted other clues that showed the dog had passed by. There was a patch of golden fur on a prickly bush, and a garden gate that was marked by the deep gash of claws. The lower branch of

a tree had been pulled off and its leaves
scattered along the pavement.

Ozzy frowned at the dark mass

of trees on the other side of the road. "I can hear something! I think it's coming from over there."

"That's the park," Kitty told him. "It's quite big, with a lake and a playground."

The night breeze lifted the leaves on the trees, making them flutter. Kitty worked hard to use all her super senses. There was a strange rustling sound— too loud to be the wind—and an odd smell drifted over the park wall, like mud mixed with chocolate.

"Let's get a little closer. But we should be careful. This dog is acting very strangely," Kitty said.

The park gate was locked, so Kitty climbed the high wall and pulled Ozzy up beside her. The owl boy crouched on the brick wall, moving his head slowly from side to side as he scanned the bushes and trees.

The park was full of cracklings and rustlings, and tree shadows stretched across the grass like long, crooked fingers. The lake at the center of the trees glinted as the moon came out from behind a cloud. "I don't like this,"

quavered Pumpkin.

"Stay here!" Kitty told the kitten. "I'll call you when we know it's safe."

Pumpkin nodded and settled on the wall, curling his little ginger tail around his body.

"Let's split up," suggested Ozzy. "Olive and I will head to the other side of the lake. Whoever finds the dog first can call the others."

"Good idea!" Kitty jumped down and

creeped through the undergrowth with Katsumi close behind her. Ozzy spread his cape wide and glided away through the trees.

"I'll check this way, Kitty," whispered Katsumi, pointing to a small path that led away to the left.

Kitty nodded and tiptoed on a little farther. Her catlike powers let her move noiselessly through the bushes and her special nighttime vision helped her notice every tiny movement.

A-ROOOO! A howl filled the air

and the sad, lonely noise made Kitty shiver. Who was this strange, wild dog, and what was he doing all alone in the dark?

Chapter 4

Kitty followed a trail of broken branches that led across the grass. Then she climbed a tall tree, hoping to get a better view of the park. A sudden growling noise came from the middle of a bramble patch, and Kitty spotted something in the shadows, roaming backward and forward.

Kitty shivered. The shadowy shape looked huge and monster-like. Then she reminded herself what her mom always said: *Remember, Kitty, you're braver than you think!*

Just as the shape came out of the bushes, a cloud hid the moon and the park sank into darkness. By the time Kitty focused with her nighttime vision, the shape had disappeared. Kitty was about to climb down from

the tree when she heard Katsumi.

"Kitty, over here!" Her friend's voice came from high in the treetops.

Kitty ran along a branch and leaped gracefully through the leaves. The wind gusted strongly, but she balanced on the swaying branch before somersaulting to

the next tree.
Peering through
the darkness, she spotted
Katsumi's bright fur. The tabby
cat was poised on the branch of an
old oak tree close to the picnic area.

"Are you all right?" called Kitty.

"Yes, I'm fine," replied Katsumi.
"The dog chased me up here—he
was quite terrifying."

Kitty swiftly climbed across to

her friend. "Why is he acting like this? It makes no sense."

Katsumi shook her head. "He seems like a very strange creature! His eyes looked wild, and his coat was covered in twigs and leaves and big lumps of chocolate cake."

"Did you talk to him?" asked Kitty.

"I tried to, but he drowned me out with his howling," Katsumi told her. "Then he chased me through the bushes. I escaped by climbing this tree, and I thought I'd wait here to see what he did next."

"I'm going to get closer and see what he's doing." Kitty climbed swiftly down the trunk and looked around. The bushes on the other side of the

picnic area were rustling, and there was a sharp whimpering sound.

Kitty creeped across the grass, past the picnic benches, her eyes fixed on the shaking bushes. The dog was thrashing wildly and breaking the branches.

Kitty's heart thumped, and she took a deep breath to try to stay calm. "Stop right there!"

she cried. "My name is Kitty, and I'm a superhero in training! Come out of that bush right now! You have a lot of explaining to do."

The dog barked loudly, and his thrashing grew even wilder. Leaves and twigs and bits of moss flew into the air. Kitty's eyes widened in alarm, and she got ready to leap out of the way in case the dog came charging straight at her.

At last the creature broke through the branches. Kitty jumped back, but the dog just slumped on the ground in front of her with a whimper. "I'm sorry! I know I've been a bad, *bad* dog."

"You've certainly had us running all over the place to find you." Kitty hesitated. Then she crouched down beside the creature. He was a beautiful golden Labrador, but leaves and

mud were stuck to his coat, along with dollops of chocolate mousse.

The dog gave a long groan and covered his eyes with one paw. Kitty saw his tail drooping and felt sorry for him in spite of all the trouble he'd caused. "I'm Kitty," she told him again. "What's your name?"

"I'm Ludo, and I live at the Sticky Bun bakery. The humans that live there came to the stray animal home and picked me to be their dog. They're really nice to me and . . ." He broke off with a sob.

Kitty looked at him in surprise. "If you like it there, then why did you make such a mess?"

Ludo broke into another howl, and Kitty patted his head. "Shh! Why don't you tell me what's wrong? Maybe I can help."

"They bought me a shiny leather collar with the bakery's address and telephone number written in gold letters," cried Ludo. "But it was a bit loose and it must have come off somewhere!"

He sniffed before continuing. "I

looked all over the shop and the bakery's kitchen, but I couldn't find it. Then I came out here, because this is where we went for a walk today!" He jumped up and looked around wildly. "It *must* be here somewhere! I can't go back without it or my owners will think I don't want to be their dog after all."

He began pawing at the earth and the

bushes, covering himself and Kitty in twigs and leaves.

"Stop! I'll help you find it—I promise," Kitty told him. "We can look together."

Ludo's sad eyes lit up. "Really? You don't mind helping me?"

Kitty smiled. "Of course not. My friends will help too." Katsumi stepped gracefully through the bushes. "Katsumi—this is Ludo, and he's sad because he lost the collar his new owners gave him. I told him we'd help."

Ludo looked ashamed. "I'm sorry I

chased you before! I was trying to explain, but everything came out wrong."

"That's all right." Katsumi turned to Kitty. "Maybe we should call Ozzy and Olive."

"Good idea." Kitty looked around. Where was Ozzy? She hadn't seen him since they split up to search in different directions.

Just then, there was a clear hooting sound. *Tu-WIT! Tu-WOO!*

"That must be Ozzy," explained Kitty. "Let's go and meet him. His owl powers give him amazing eyesight, so he'll be really helpful for finding your collar."

Ludo, Kitty, and Katsumi dashed through the trees and on to the path that ran beside the lake. Then Kitty stopped suddenly.

Ozzy was standing there with Olive perched on his shoulder. Beside him was a golden Labrador who looked *exactly* the same as

Ludo. Except this dog was also wearing a shiny leather collar.

Chapter

5

Ozzy grinned widely. "I've found the dog from the bakery. His name is Tully, and he's sorry he made such a mess . . ." He broke off, staring at Ludo. "Who's that?"

Ludo sprang at Tully, barking loudly. "That's my collar! Give it back!"

Kitty pulled Ludo away. "Wait a minute—*this* is the dog from the bakery," she said to Ozzy. "He's been running around looking for his lost collar."

Ozzy looked from Ludo to Tully and frowned.

"That's not true! It's my collar," said Tully. "I'm the one who lives in the bakery, and this dog is just fibbing!"

Ozzy's frown faded. "See? This is the bakery dog. Maybe this other one got into the shop and caused all the mess because he was hungry."

Kitty looked into Ludo's sad brown eyes. She felt a tingling—like an extra sense—that what he'd told her was true. He would never have been so upset about losing the collar if it was all a lie. "I know it's confusing, but I'm *sure* that

Ludo is the real bakery dog," she began.

"I don't think so!" Ozzy folded his arms. "Your dog doesn't even have a collar. He's probably a stray."

"I did have a collar," howled Ludo. "Then I lost it!"

Kitty folded her arms, too. "Actually, he's explained it all to me—how his collar was loose and how he's worried

his owners might be upset that he's lost it. I really believe him!"

"You're so sure you're right all the time!" Ozzy looked annoyed. "You're not the only one with superpowers anymore, you know."

Kitty turned red. Ozzy was the one who was acting like *he* was right all the time. "This is silly! There's no point arguing about it . . ." She stared at the two dogs, her forehead creasing.

Pumpkin scampered up and brushed against Kitty's legs. "What's happening? I heard all the shouting and thought I should come and help." He looked nervously at the two dogs.

Olive ruffled her feathers. "Both these dogs are saying they belong at

the bakery. But one of them must be making it up."

"If only there was a way to tell which one," Katsumi said, swishing her tail thoughtfully.

Kitty gazed at Tully's collar. The leather looked new and shiny, and the bakery's name, address, and telephone number were spelled out in gold letters. "I know! Tell me the phone number

of the bakery written on that collar."

Tully stuck his nose in

the air. "I don't know. I've never read it!"

Ludo wagged his tail. "That's easy!" And he reeled off the number perfectly.

Ozzy leaned closer to read the collar before glaring at Tully. "You haven't been telling the truth!"

Tully laughed nastily. "Who cares? We look the same, and the owners of the bakery will never tell the difference." With a growl, he leaped out of Ozzy's reach. "He's not getting the collar back! He shouldn't have lost it in the first place."

"That's really mean!" Ozzy made a grab for Tully, but he darted out of the way again.

"No, it's not!" the dog snapped back. "Why should he get the chance to live

in that nice, cozy place instead of me?"
Then he galloped away across the park
and disappeared behind the trees.

"Don't let him get away!" howled
Ludo.

"Don't worry—we can stop him," Kitty said. "But it's going to take teamwork."

Ozzy nodded. "Let's spread out and cover different sides of the park. Olive and I can go to the main gate."

"That's a good idea," said Kitty. "Katsumi and Ludo, you cover the exit near the corner shop. Pumpkin and I will go to the left-hand corner where there's a gap in the fence. Together, we'll catch him!"

They raced away through the

trees. Kitty ran faster than
ever, leaping over benches and
bushes. She stopped by the gap in
the fence, all her superpowers
on full alert. Pumpkin crouched
beside her. Kitty heard a tree
creaking in the wind. Then a
mouse scuttled through the
fallen leaves.

Suddenly, there was a
scuffling noise from the

direction of the lake, followed by three owl hoots. That must be Ozzy calling her! "I'm coming!" she cried, racing toward the sound.

Ozzy was charging along the lakeside, trying to reach the escaping Tully. The dog barked wildly and ran even faster, so Ozzy pulled off his owl cape and threw it into the air. The cloak spiraled through the dark, landing right on top of Tully. The

dog fell to the ground, twisting and squirming beneath the cape.

Ozzy dusted his hands together proudly. "I caught him! Now we can get that collar back."

Just then, Tully wrenched himself free. Ozzy leaped back in surprise, and Tully staggered forward, tumbling over the bank into the lake with a huge splash. "Help, I can't swim!" He thrashed around in the water.

Kitty sprang forward, but the dog had already floated out of reach. "Don't worry! I'll rescue you." She swung herself into a tree and darted along a

branch that hung over the
water. Reaching down, she grabbed
Tully's collar and hauled him out of
the lake. The dog fell onto the bank,
shivering and looking very sorry for
himself.

Kitty leaped to the ground and undid the collar before giving it to Ludo. Then she took off her cape and wrapped it around Tully to stop him from shivering.

Tully sniffed and looked at Ludo sadly. "I know I shouldn't have kept the collar . . . but I wanted a home of my own so badly! When I saw you out for a walk with your owners, I wished it was me—with a good home and people who love me! Then I saw the collar on the ground . . . and I took it."

"I'm sorry you've been lonely." Kitty

crouched down beside him. "Ozzy and
I are superheroes in training, so maybe
we could help?"

"Everyone deserves a good home,"
added Ludo, eagerly. "It was the stray

animal center that helped me to find one. They're very nice people!"

"That's a wonderful idea!" said Kitty. "We can take you to see them tonight."

Tully jumped up and wagged his tail. Then he and Ludo touched noses.

"Sorry, Ludo," said Tully.

"I'm glad we're friends now." Ludo wagged his tail too.

"So everything's sorted out at last," said Pumpkin, stretching sleepily. "It was so much easier when we worked together."

Ozzy grinned at Kitty. "I think we make quite a good team. Two superheroes are definitely better than one!"

Kitty smiled back. "I think you're right!"

Chapter
6

Katsumi suggested cleaning the bakery before taking Tully to the animal center, so they headed back there and worked hard to make the place perfect again. Olive picked up raisins with her beak while Katsumi and Pumpkin pushed a cleaning cloth around the counters.

Ozzy mixed up some ingredients and made a cake to replace the broken one with the lemon-colored icing.

"That looks delicious!" said Kitty admiringly.

"I really like making cakes," Ozzy told her. "It's a shame we can't try a bit of this one."

"You could take some of these leftover cupcakes instead." Ludo pointed to a row of cakes with swirly frosting. "I heard Mrs. Gallo say they needed to be eaten up!"

Kitty packed a few cupcakes into a paper bag and checked that the whole bakery was sparkling and clean. Then they said good-bye to Ludo before walking down the road to the stray animal home.

Kitty kneeled down beside Tully and hugged him gently. "Good luck, Tully! I hope you can come and visit me once you've been given a new home."

"Thank you for everything, and I'm

sorry for the trouble I caused. I hope my new owners are kind like you two."

Tully touched noses with Kitty and then with Ozzy before trotting through the gates of the animal center.

Kitty sighed. "I hope it doesn't take too long to find him a good owner. Everyone needs a place that feels like home."

Ozzy nodded. "Moving to Hallam City was really strange and scary. At first I didn't feel like I belonged here, but now that I've found someone else

who's like me, it's not such a bad place
after all!"

Kitty linked arms with him. "Let's go
home and eat those cupcakes!"

By the time they reached the tree house, Kitty couldn't stop rubbing her tired eyes. She performed the final leap across to the old oak tree with Pumpkin lying on her shoulders already fast asleep. Olive's wings drooped as she perched on the windowsill of the tree house, and even Katsumi was yawning widely.

Kitty pulled the comforter over her legs, handing a cupcake to Ozzy. "I think that was a job

well done!" she said. "Ludo got his collar back, and now Tully has the chance for a home of his own."

Ozzy took a bite of cupcake. "So tell me about your other adventures, Kitty."

"Only if you tell me yours, too!" said Kitty, grinning.

So Kitty told Ozzy all about her cat crew and the adventures they often had together by the light of the moon. Then Ozzy told her about the little village where he'd lived and all the owl friends he'd made there.

"I'd like to get to know more of the owls that live here in the city."

He paused, his eyes brightening as a chorus of faint hoots echoed across the rooftops. He brushed the cupcake crumbs off his fingers, before jumping to his feet.

Olive's ears pricked up, too. "The other owls are calling for you, Ozzy!"

Ozzy leaned out of the window and gave two long hoots. A minute later, three owls swooped down to settle on a branch outside the tree house. One was a barn owl with a

round, white face and brown feathers, the second was a tawny owl with speckled wings, and the last one was a long-eared owl with wide yellow eyes.

"Then it's true-hoo," said the barn owl. "A boy with owl-like powers has

come to Hallam City!"
"We heard all about your adventure
in the park," hooted the tawny owl.
"We're very good at silent flying,
and we'd love to help you on your
next nighttime mission," added the
long-eared owl.

Ozzy flushed happily. "I'd love that, too!"

"Now you'll have your own owl squad, just like my cat crew," said Kitty, beaming.

The owls settled down to roost on the roof of the tree house while Kitty snuggled down with Katsumi and Pumpkin. The stars twinkled in the velvet-black sky and the wind gently rustled the leaves of the oak tree.

Kitty sighed happily and closed her eyes. Having superpowers was amazing fun, but it was going to be even better now that she had someone to share it with!

Super Facts About Cats

Super Speed

Have you ever seen a cat make a quick escape
from a dog? If so, you know they can move
really fast—up to thirty miles per hour!

Super Hearing

Cats have an incredible sense of
hearing and can swivel their ears to
pinpoint even the tiniest of sounds.

Super Reflexes

Have you ever heard the saying, "Cats
always land on their feet"? People say this
because cats have amazing reflexes. If a cat

112

is falling, it can quickly sense how
to move its body into the right position
to land safely.

Super Vision

Cats have amazing nighttime vision. Their
incredible ability to see in low light allows
them to hunt for prey when it's dark outside.

Super Smell

Cats have a very powerful sense of smell.
Did you know that the pattern of ridges on
each cat's nose is as unique as a human's
fingerprints?

The Kitty books— read them all!

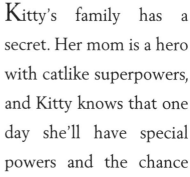

Kitty's family has a secret. Her mom is a hero with catlike superpowers, and Kitty knows that one day she'll have special powers and the chance to use them, too. That day comes sooner than expected, when a friendly black cat named Figaro comes to Kitty's bedroom window to ask for help. But the world at night is a scary place— is Kitty brave enough to step out into the darkness for a thrilling moonlight adventure?

Kitty can't wait to see the priceless Golden Tiger Statue with her own eyes. Legend says that if you hold the statue, you can make your greatest wish come true. Kitty and her cat, Pumpkin, decide to sneak into the museum to see the statue at night, when no one else is around. But disaster strikes when the statue is stolen right in front of them! Can Kitty find the thief and return the precious statue before sunrise?

Kitty, Pumpkin, and Pixie discover a sky garden hidden high on a rooftop. It's a magical place, filled with beautiful flowers and sparkling fairy lights. Pixie is so excited, she wants to tell everyone about it—but the more cats discover the sky garden, the wilder it becomes! Soon the rooftop is overrun with unwelcome visitors. Can Kitty and her friends protect this secret, special place—and all the magical things growing in it—before it's too late?

Meowing Soon!